Robin and Sally stories
Stage 7

Name

Read and do.

Draw a cricket bat in the girl's hand.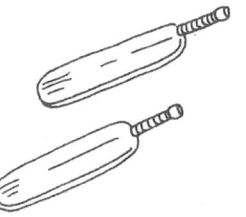

Draw a cricket bat in Dad's hand.

Draw a cricket ball on the grass.

Draw a bird in the tree.

Draw the sun in the sky.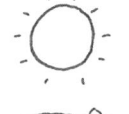

Draw Moggy on the wall.

Heinemann

The cricket bat mystery

Skill: Reading and following instructions
Instructions: Read the sentences and then complete the picture.

Answer the questions.

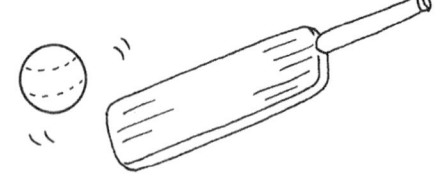

What did Robin ask Mum? (page 3)

What did Mum say? (page 3)

How did the girl say she got the bat? (page 8)

What did Sally say when she looked at the girl's bat? (page 11)

Why did Dad put Robin's bat in the shed? (page 15)

What did Robin say to the girl? (page 16)

What did the girl say to Robin? (page 16)

The cricket bat mystery

Skill: Comprehension
Instructions: Answer the questions. Look back at the story to help you. When you have finished discuss your answers with a partner.

Write the sentence.

Sally and Robin

The boy said, '

Sally and the boy

The boy

Moggy

The boy pulled on

The boy said, '

The new boy

Skill: Reading for meaning
Instructions: Complete the sentences by rearranging the word order so that they make sense. Remember to use a full stop at the end of each sentence.

Circle the blend.

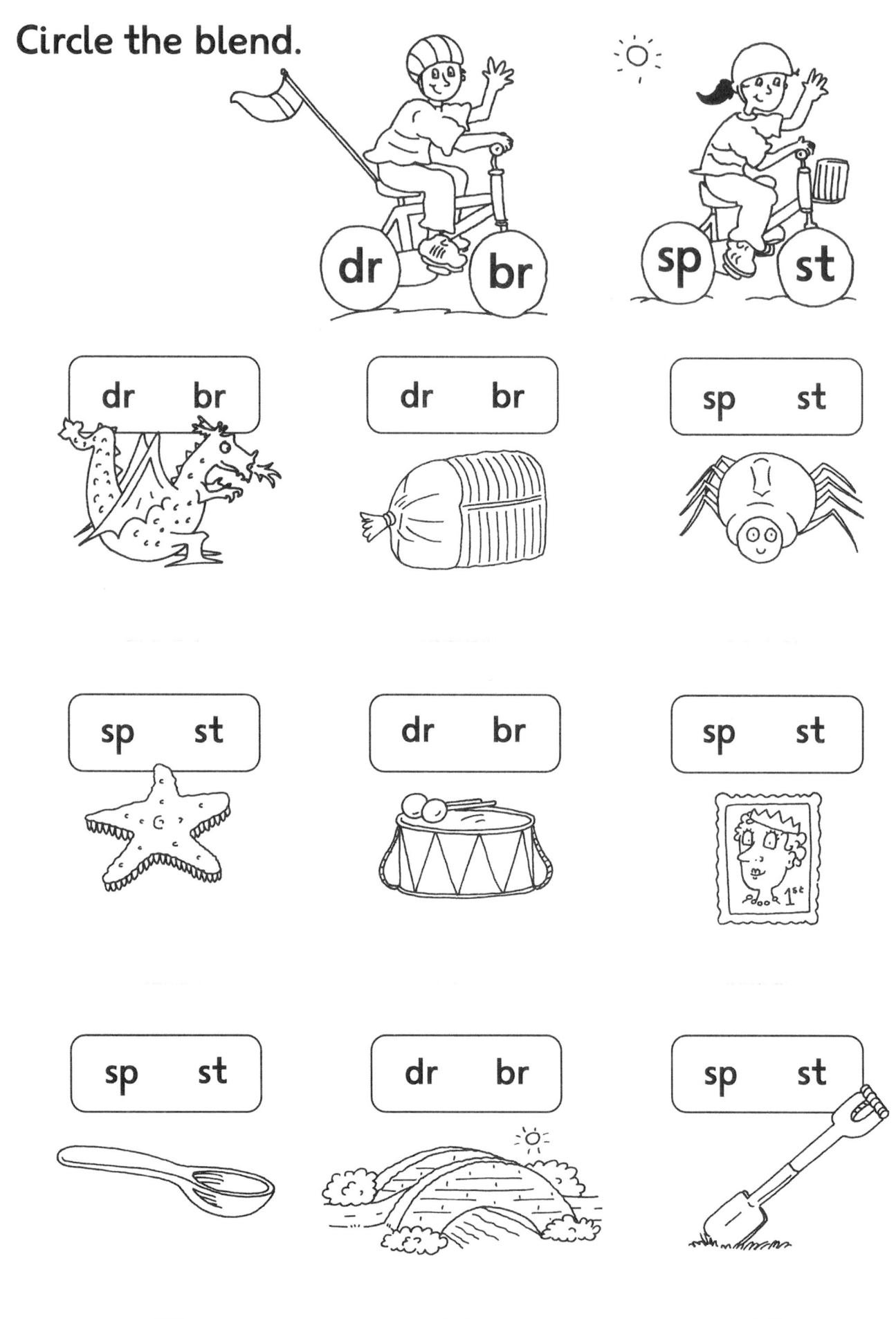

The new boy

Skill: Identifying initial blends which have one consonant in common
Instructions: Circle the correct blend above each picture and then write the blend under the picture.

Match the words.

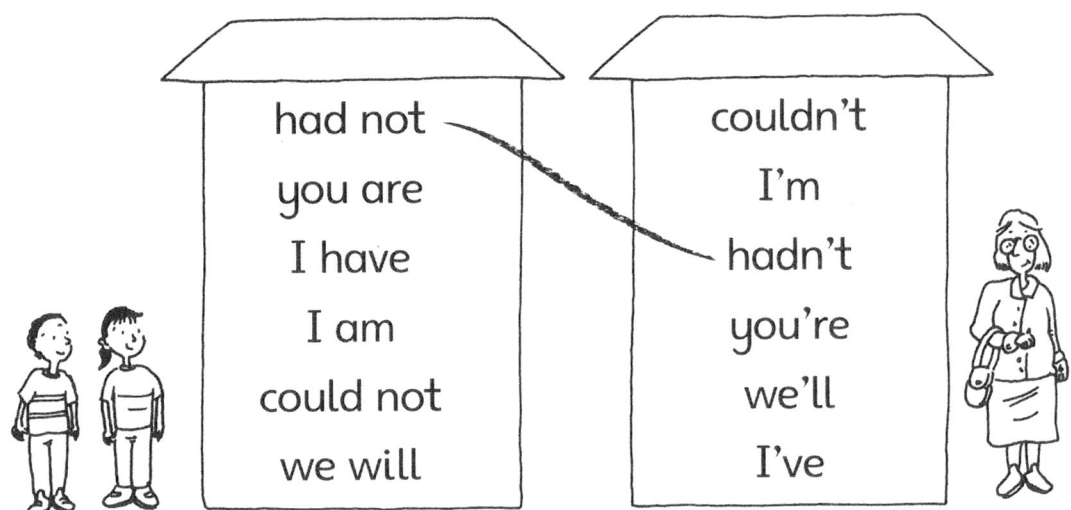

had not	couldn't
you are	I'm
I have	hadn't
I am	you're
could not	we'll
we will	I've

(had not — hadn't)

Make two words into one word.

'I am coming to get you,' said Sally.

Robin saw Mrs Brown but he just could not stop.

'What do you think you are doing?' said Mrs Brown.

'I fell over the rug and I have hurt my leg,' said Mrs Brown.

'We will go and get our mum,' called Robin.

'If you had not come to see Mrs Brown she could have been on the floor all night,' said the policewoman.

The next door neighbour

Skill: Using the apostrophe to mark missing letters
Instructions: Join the two words to the correct contraction. Then write the correct contraction under the two words.

Change the odd word.

Robin didn't see cold Mrs Brown walking up the path.

He couldn't hop and he pushed her into the fence.

'My don't you look where you're going?' she said.

Mum said, 'Why don't you go and say lorry again?'

Cut Mrs Brown didn't come to the door.

Robin paw Mrs Brown on the rug by the TV.

She said, 'I fell over the rug and I've curt my leg.'

Robin called to his mum, 'Mrs Brown bell over.'

Mum said, 'I'll ball for help.'

An ambulance book Mrs Brown to hospital.

The next door neighbour

Skill: Reading for meaning
Instructions: Read the sentences and underline the odd word. Then write the correct word on the line.

Fill in the gaps.

been asked next after took because with
lots must came cross When have please

One day Gran _____ over to see Robin and Sally.

'Will you look _____ Bouncer for me?' she asked.

'Oh, _____ say yes, Mum!' said Robin and Sally.

Mum said, 'You will _____ to look after him.'

Sally and Robin _____ Bouncer for a walk in the park.

The _____ day Robin didn't want to walk Bouncer _____ it was too cold.

So Mum had to go for a walk _____ Bouncer.

Mum was _____. 'If you have a dog you _____ look after it,' she said.

So Sally and Robin took Bouncer for _____ of walks.

_____ Gran came to get Bouncer, Mum said, 'Robin and Sally have _____ very good.'

Robin and Sally _____ Mum, 'Can we have a dog now?'

Bouncer comes to stay

Skill: Reading comprehension – cloze
Instructions: Look back at the story and complete the sentences using the words from the box.

Make the words.

ip
ag
op

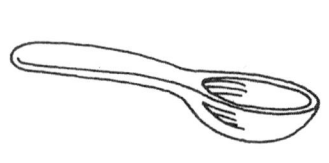
ot
ell
in

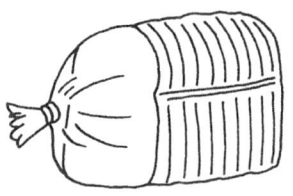
ing
ick
ush

op
ep
ill

Bouncer comes to stay

Skill: Identifying initial blends which have one consonant in common
Instructions: Write the blend next to the picture. Then use the blend and endings to make words and write the words twice.

Robin and Sally stories
Stage 7

Name

Read and do.

Draw a cricket bat in the girl's hand.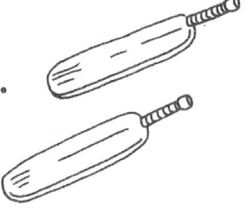

Draw a cricket bat in Dad's hand.

Draw a cricket ball on the grass.

Draw a bird in the tree.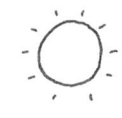

Draw the sun in the sky.

Draw Moggy on the wall.

The cricket bat mystery

Skill: Reading and following instructions
Instructions: Read the sentences and then complete the picture.

Answer the questions.

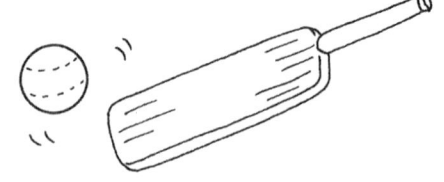

What did Robin ask Mum? (page 3)

What did Mum say? (page 3)

How did the girl say she got the bat? (page 8)

What did Sally say when she looked at the girl's bat? (page 11)

Why did Dad put Robin's bat in the shed? (page 15)

What did Robin say to the girl? (page 16)

What did the girl say to Robin? (page 16)

The cricket bat mystery

Skill: Comprehension
Instructions: Answer the questions. Look back at the story to help you. When you have finished discuss your answers with a partner.

Write the sentence.

Sally and Robin

The boy said, '

Sally and the boy

The boy

Moggy

The boy pulled on

The boy said, '

The new boy

Skill: Reading for meaning
Instructions: Complete the sentences by rearranging the word order so that they make sense. Remember to use a full stop at the end of each sentence.

Circle the blend.

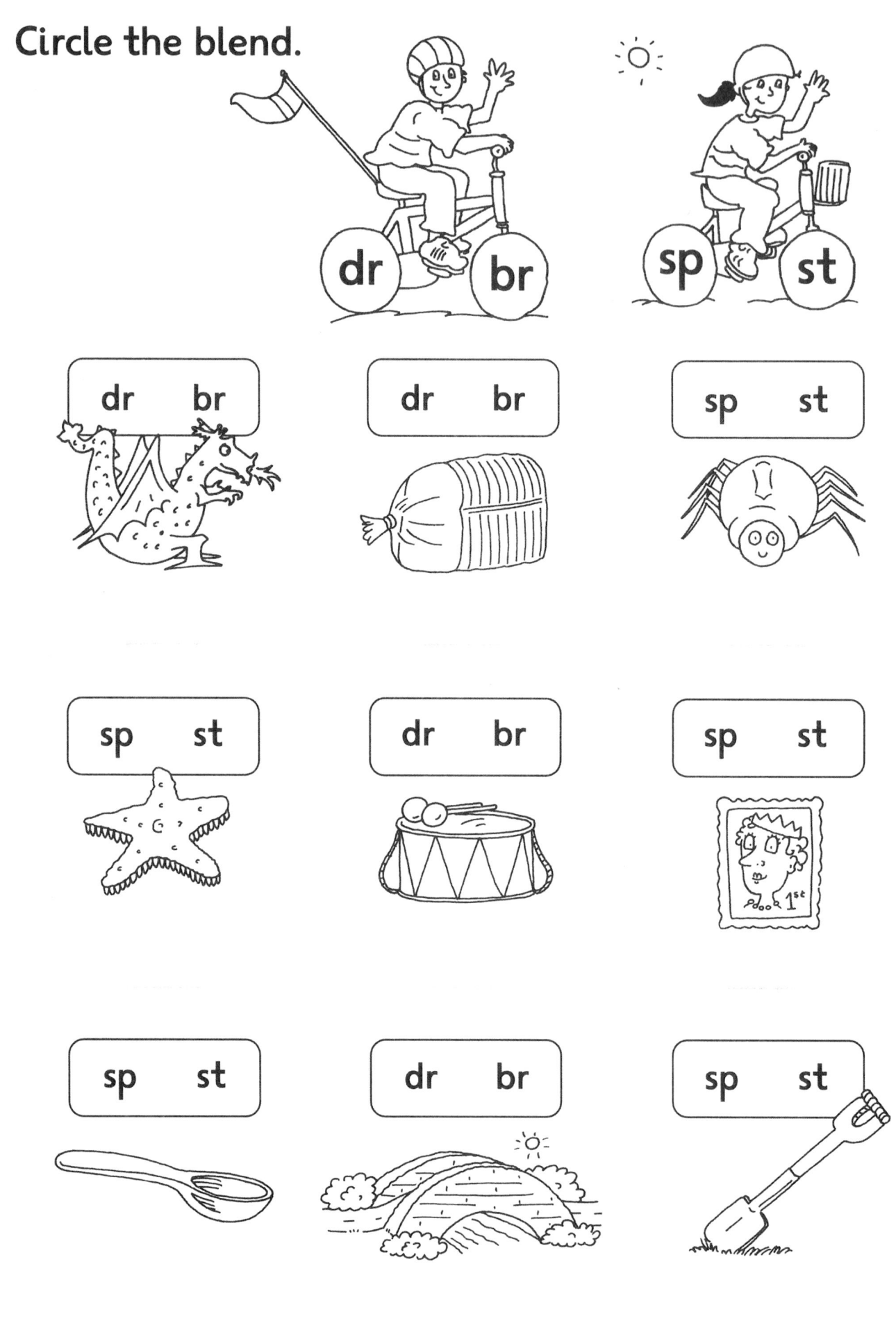

The new boy

Skill: Identifying initial blends which have one consonant in common
Instructions: Circle the correct blend above each picture and then write the blend under the picture.

Match the words.

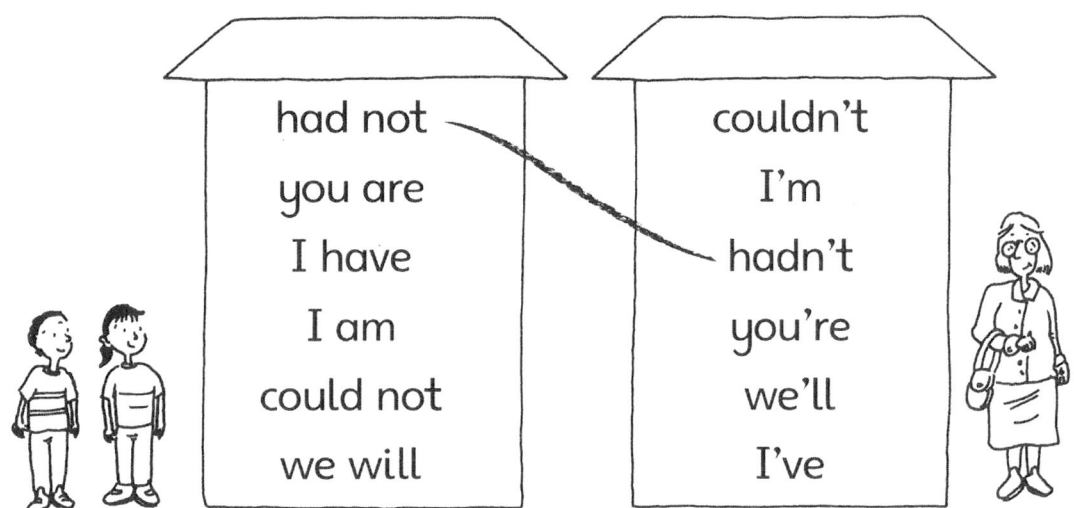

had not — hadn't
you are
I have
I am
could not
we will

couldn't
I'm
hadn't
you're
we'll
I've

Make two words into one word.

'I am coming to get you,' said Sally.

Robin saw Mrs Brown but he just could not stop.

'What do you think you are doing?' said Mrs Brown.

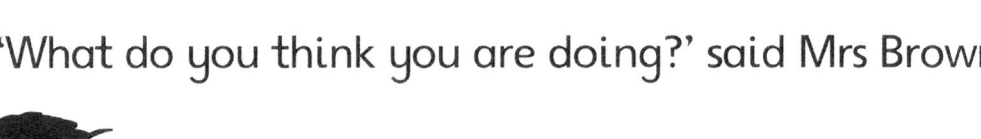

'I fell over the rug and I have hurt my leg,' said Mrs Brown.

'We will go and get our mum,' called Robin.

'If you had not come to see Mrs Brown she could

have been on the floor all night,' said the policewoman.

The next door neighbour

Skill: Using the apostrophe to mark missing letters
Instructions: Join the two words to the correct contraction. Then write the correct contraction under the two words.

Change the odd word.

Robin didn't see cold Mrs Brown walking up the path.

He couldn't hop and he pushed her into the fence.

'My don't you look where you're going?' she said.

Mum said, 'Why don't you go and say lorry again?'

Cut Mrs Brown didn't come to the door.

Robin paw Mrs Brown on the rug by the TV.

She said, 'I fell over the rug and I've curt my leg.'

Robin called to his mum, 'Mrs Brown bell over.'

Mum said, 'I'll ball for help.'

An ambulance book Mrs Brown to hospital.

The next door neighbour

Skill: Reading for meaning
Instructions: Read the sentences and underline the odd word. Then write the correct word on the line.

Fill in the gaps.

been   asked   next   after   took   because   with
lots   must   came   cross   When   have   please

One day Gran _____ over to see Robin and Sally.

'Will you look _____ Bouncer for me?' she asked.

'Oh, _____ say yes, Mum!' said Robin and Sally.

Mum said, 'You will _____ to look after him.'

Sally and Robin _____ Bouncer for a walk in the park.

The _____ day Robin didn't want to walk Bouncer _____ it was too cold.

So Mum had to go for a walk _____ Bouncer.

Mum was _____. 'If you have a dog you _____ look after it,' she said.

So Sally and Robin took Bouncer for _____ of walks.

_____ Gran came to get Bouncer, Mum said, 'Robin and Sally have _____ very good.'

Robin and Sally _____ Mum, 'Can we have a dog now?'

Bouncer comes to stay

Skill: Reading comprehension – cloze
Instructions: Look back at the story and complete the sentences using the words from the box.

Make the words.

ip
ag
op

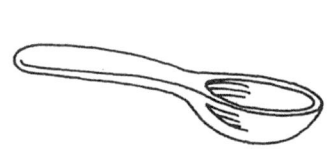
ot
ell
in

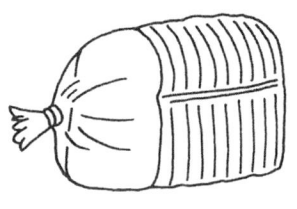
ing
ick
ush

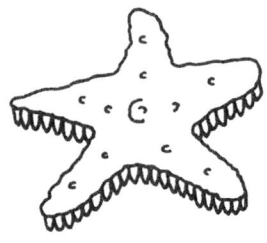
op
ep
ill

Bouncer comes to stay

Skill: Identifying initial blends which have one consonant in common
Instructions: Write the blend next to the picture. Then use the blend and endings to make words and write the words twice.

Robin and Sally stories Stage 7

Name

Read and do.

Draw a cricket bat in the girl's hand.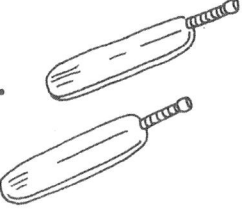

Draw a cricket bat in Dad's hand.

Draw a cricket ball on the grass.

Draw a bird in the tree.

Draw the sun in the sky.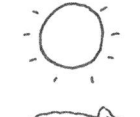

Draw Moggy on the wall.

The cricket bat mystery

Skill: Reading and following instructions
Instructions: Read the sentences and then complete the picture.

Answer the questions.

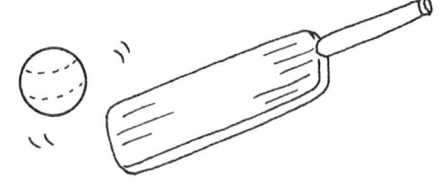

What did Robin ask Mum? (page 3)

What did Mum say? (page 3)

How did the girl say she got the bat? (page 8)

What did Sally say when she looked at the girl's bat? (page 11)

Why did Dad put Robin's bat in the shed? (page 15)

What did Robin say to the girl? (page 16)

What did the girl say to Robin? (page 16)

The cricket bat mystery

Skill: Comprehension
Instructions: Answer the questions. Look back at the story to help you. When you have finished discuss your answers with a partner.

Write the sentence.

Sally and Robin

The boy said, '

Sally and the boy

The boy

Moggy

The boy pulled on

The boy said, '

The new boy

Skill: Reading for meaning
Instructions: Complete the sentences by rearranging the word order so that they make sense. Remember to use a full stop at the end of each sentence.

Circle the blend.

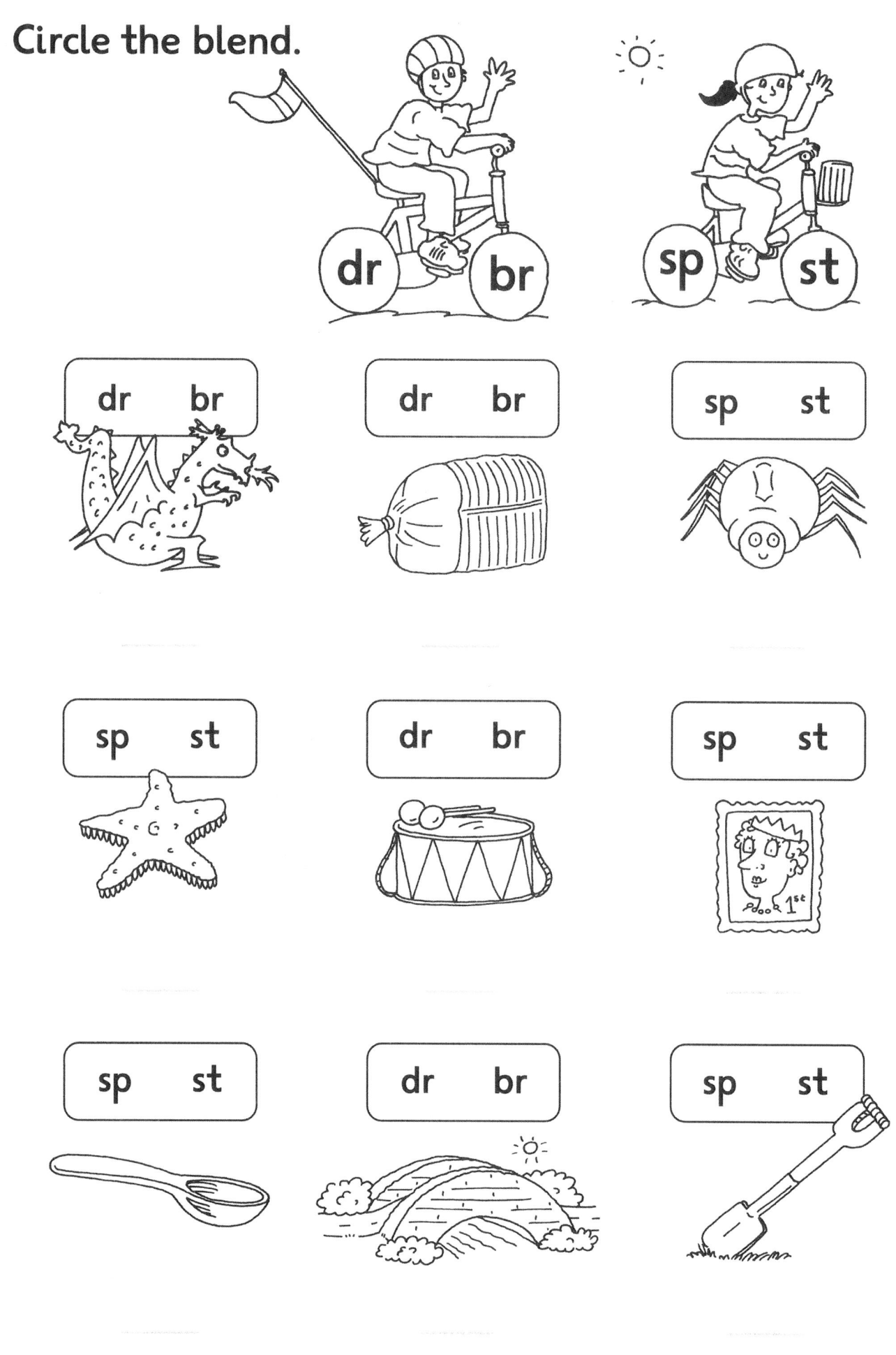

The new boy

Skill: Identifying initial blends which have one consonant in common
Instructions: Circle the correct blend above each picture and then write the blend under the picture.

Match the words.

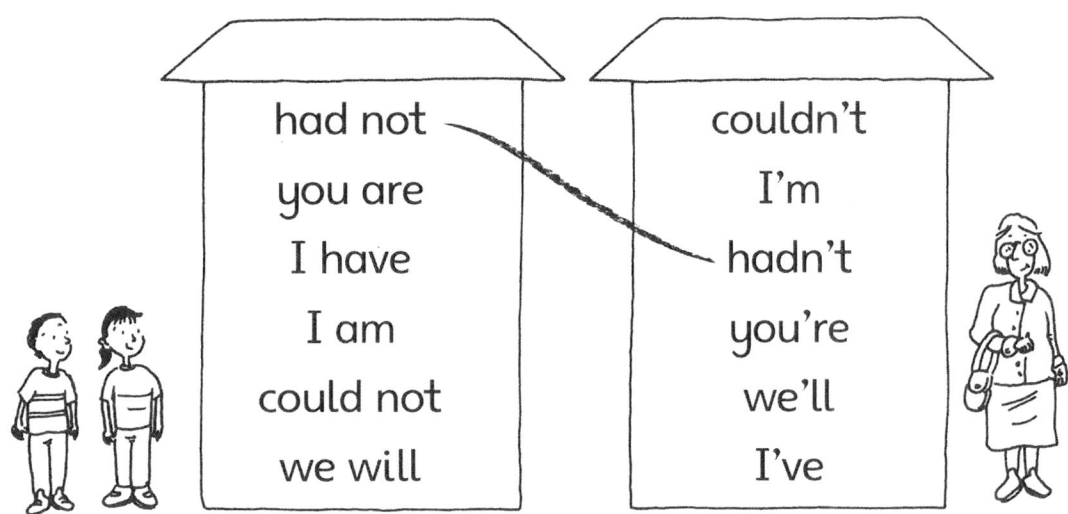

had not	couldn't
you are	I'm
I have	hadn't
I am	you're
could not	we'll
we will	I've

Make two words into one word.

'I am coming to get you,' said Sally.

Robin saw Mrs Brown but he just could not stop.

'What do you think you are doing?' said Mrs Brown.

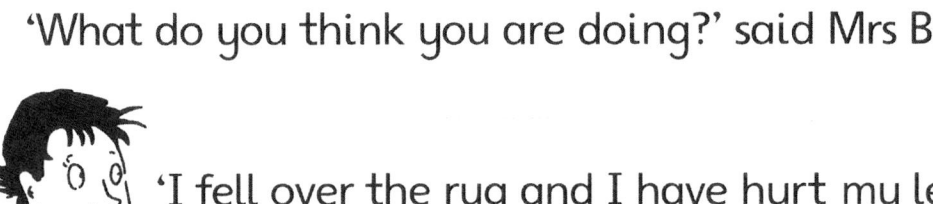

'I fell over the rug and I have hurt my leg,' said Mrs Brown.

'We will go and get our mum,' called Robin.

'If you had not come to see Mrs Brown she could

have been on the floor all night,' said the policewoman.

The next door neighbour

Skill: Using the apostrophe to mark missing letters
Instructions: Join the two words to the correct contraction. Then write the correct contraction under the two words.

Change the odd word.

Robin didn't see cold Mrs Brown walking up the path.

He couldn't hop and he pushed her into the fence.

'My don't you look where you're going?' she said.

Mum said, 'Why don't you go and say lorry again?'

Cut Mrs Brown didn't come to the door.

Robin paw Mrs Brown on the rug by the TV.

She said, 'I fell over the rug and I've curt my leg.'

Robin called to his mum, 'Mrs Brown bell over.'

Mum said, 'I'll ball for help.'

An ambulance book Mrs Brown to hospital.

The next door neighbour

Skill: Reading for meaning
Instructions: Read the sentences and underline the odd word. Then write the correct word on the line.

Fill in the gaps.

been   asked   next   after   took   because   with
lots   must   came   cross   When   have   please

One day Gran _____ over to see Robin and Sally.

'Will you look _____ Bouncer for me?' she asked.

'Oh, _____ say yes, Mum!' said Robin and Sally.

Mum said, 'You will _____ to look after him.'

Sally and Robin _____ Bouncer for a walk in the park.

The _____ day Robin didn't want to walk Bouncer _____ it was too cold.

So Mum had to go for a walk _____ Bouncer.

Mum was _____. 'If you have a dog you _____ look after it,' she said.

So Sally and Robin took Bouncer for _____ of walks.

_____ Gran came to get Bouncer, Mum said, 'Robin and Sally have _____ very good.'

Robin and Sally _____ Mum, 'Can we have a dog now?'

Bouncer comes to stay

Skill: Reading comprehension – cloze
Instructions: Look back at the story and complete the sentences using the words from the box.

Make the words.

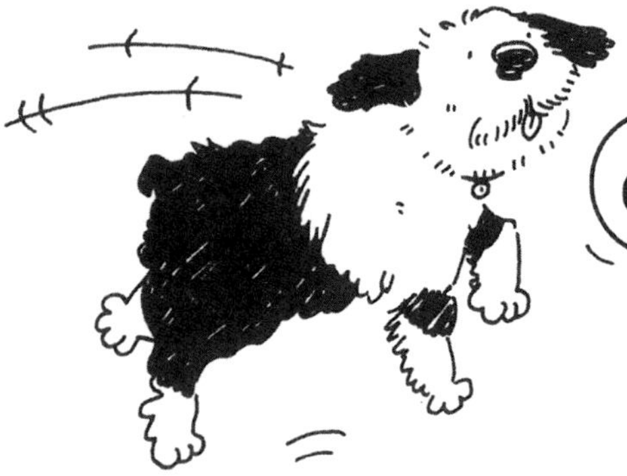

dr br sp st

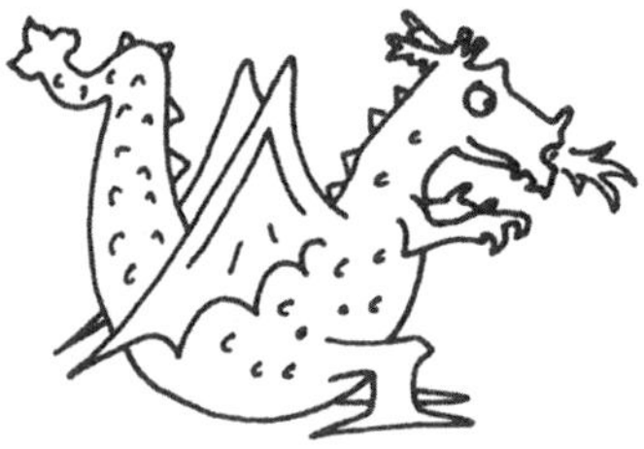

ip
ag
op

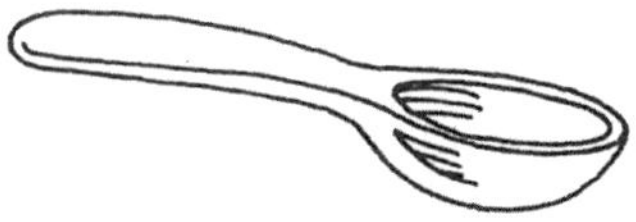

ot
ell
in

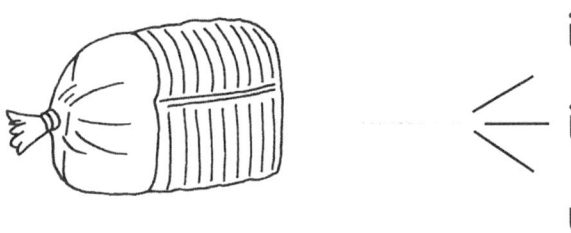

ing
ick
ush

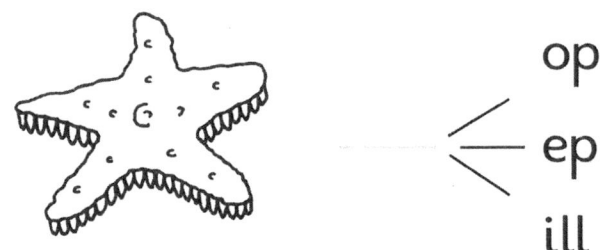

op
ep
ill

Bouncer comes to stay

Skill: Identifying initial blends which have one consonant in common
Instructions: Write the blend next to the picture. Then use the blend and endings to make words and write the words twice.

ISBN 978-0-435092-05-4
Heinemann is an imprint of Pearson Education Limited, a company incorporated in England and Wales, having its registered office at Edinburgh Gate, Harlow, Essex, CM20 2JE. Registered company number: 872828
Pack ISBN 978 0 435 09205 4 (Single ISBN 978 0 435 09193 4) © Diana Bentley and Dee Reid 1997. Illustrated by Cathy Hughes. **Printed in Great Britain by Bell and Bain Ltd** 22 27

Robin and Sally stories Stage 7

Name

Read and do.

Draw a cricket bat in the girl's hand.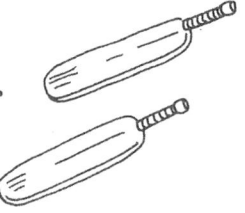

Draw a cricket bat in Dad's hand.

Draw a cricket ball on the grass.

Draw a bird in the tree.

Draw the sun in the sky.

Draw Moggy on the wall.

Heinemann

The cricket bat mystery

Skill: Reading and following instructions
Instructions: Read the sentences and then complete the picture.

Answer the questions.

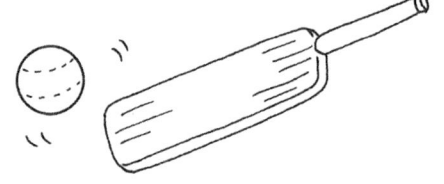

What did Robin ask Mum? (page 3)

What did Mum say? (page 3)

How did the girl say she got the bat? (page 8)

What did Sally say when she looked at the girl's bat? (page 11)

Why did Dad put Robin's bat in the shed? (page 15)

What did Robin say to the girl? (page 16)

What did the girl say to Robin? (page 16)

The cricket bat mystery

Skill: Comprehension
Instructions: Answer the questions. Look back at the story to help you. When you have finished discuss your answers with a partner.

Write the sentence.

Sally and Robin [boy a saw a van by]

The boy said, ' [with I want you don't play to] ,

Sally and the boy [bikes on their got]

The boy [fast going too Sally was much for]

Moggy [bike on didn't the his see boy coming]

The boy pulled on [Moggy away and his brakes ran]

The boy said, ' [now friends Can be we] ?'

The new boy

Skill: Reading for meaning
Instructions: Complete the sentences by rearranging the word order so that they make sense. Remember to use a full stop at the end of each sentence.

Circle the blend.

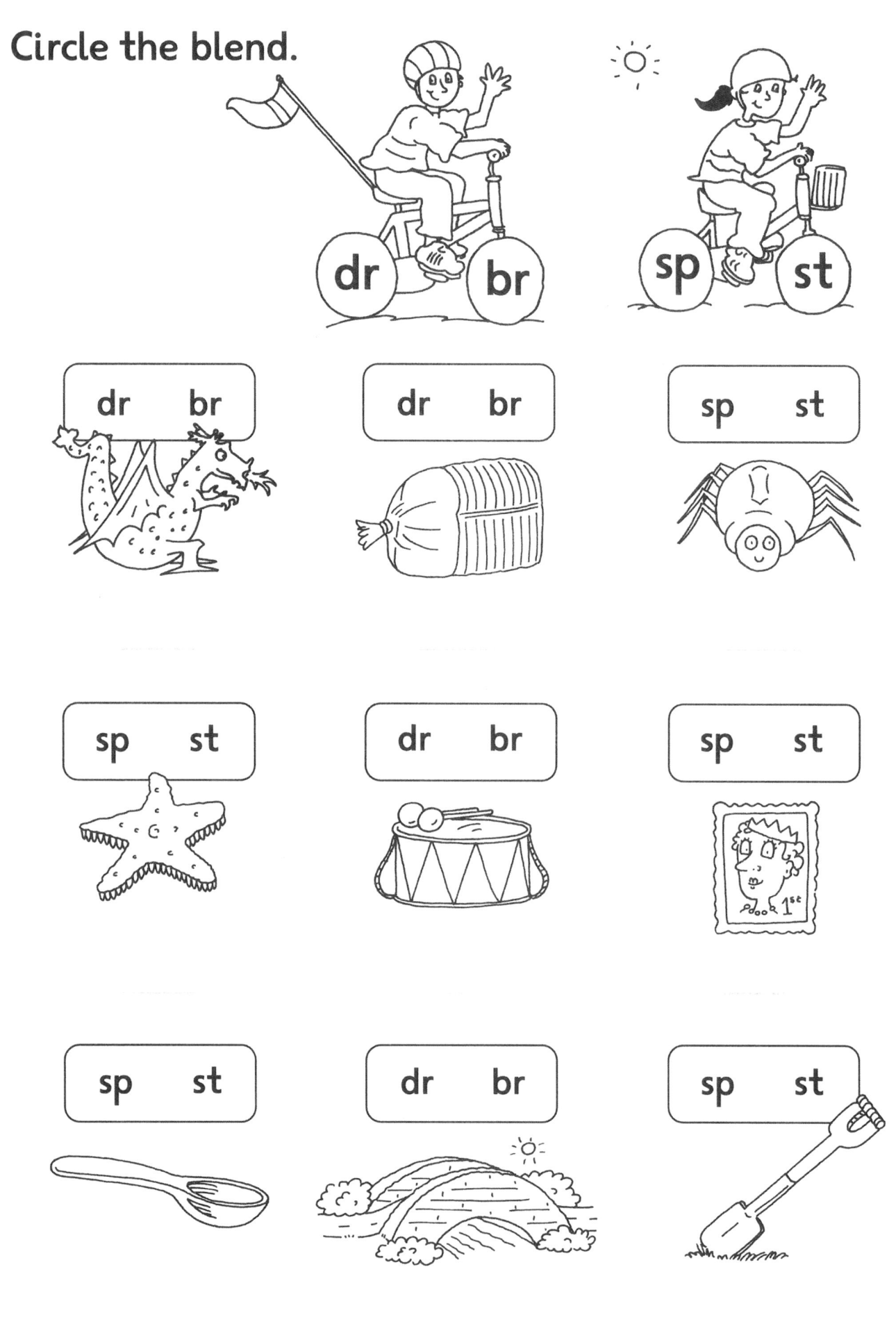

The new boy

Skill: Identifying initial blends which have one consonant in common
Instructions: Circle the correct blend above each picture and then write the blend under the picture.

Match the words.

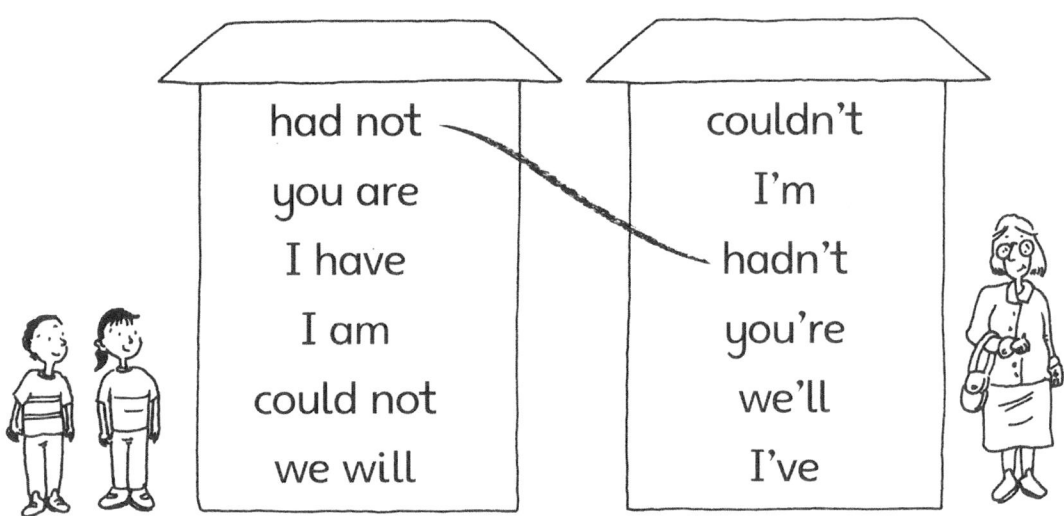

had not — couldn't
you are — I'm
I have — hadn't
I am — you're
could not — we'll
we will — I've

Make two words into one word.

'I am coming to get you,' said Sally.

Robin saw Mrs Brown but he just could not stop.

'What do you think you are doing?' said Mrs Brown.

'I fell over the rug and I have hurt my leg,' said Mrs Brown.

'We will go and get our mum,' called Robin.

'If you had not come to see Mrs Brown she could

have been on the floor all night,' said the policewoman.

The next door neighbour

Skill: Using the apostrophe to mark missing letters
Instructions: Join the two words to the correct contraction. Then write the correct contraction under the two words.

Change the odd word.

Robin didn't see cold Mrs Brown walking up the path.

He couldn't hop and he pushed her into the fence.

'My don't you look where you're going?' she said.

Mum said, 'Why don't you go and say lorry again?'

Cut Mrs Brown didn't come to the door.

Robin paw Mrs Brown on the rug by the TV.

She said, 'I fell over the rug and I've curt my leg.'

Robin called to his mum, 'Mrs Brown bell over.'

Mum said, 'I'll ball for help.'

An ambulance book Mrs Brown to hospital.

The next door neighbour

Skill: Reading for meaning
Instructions: Read the sentences and underline the odd word. Then write the correct word on the line.

Fill in the gaps.

been   asked   next   after   took   because   with
lots   must   came   cross   When   have   please

One day Gran _____ over to see Robin and Sally.

'Will you look _____ Bouncer for me?' she asked.

'Oh, _____ say yes, Mum!' said Robin and Sally.

Mum said, 'You will _____ to look after him.'

Sally and Robin _____ Bouncer for a walk in the park.

The _____ day Robin didn't want to walk Bouncer _____ it was too cold.

So Mum had to go for a walk _____ Bouncer.

Mum was _____. 'If you have a dog you _____ look after it,' she said.

So Sally and Robin took Bouncer for _____ of walks.

_____ Gran came to get Bouncer, Mum said, 'Robin and Sally have _____ very good.'

Robin and Sally _____ Mum, 'Can we have a dog now?'

Bouncer comes to stay

Skill: Reading comprehension – cloze
Instructions: Look back at the story and complete the sentences using the words from the box.

Make the words.

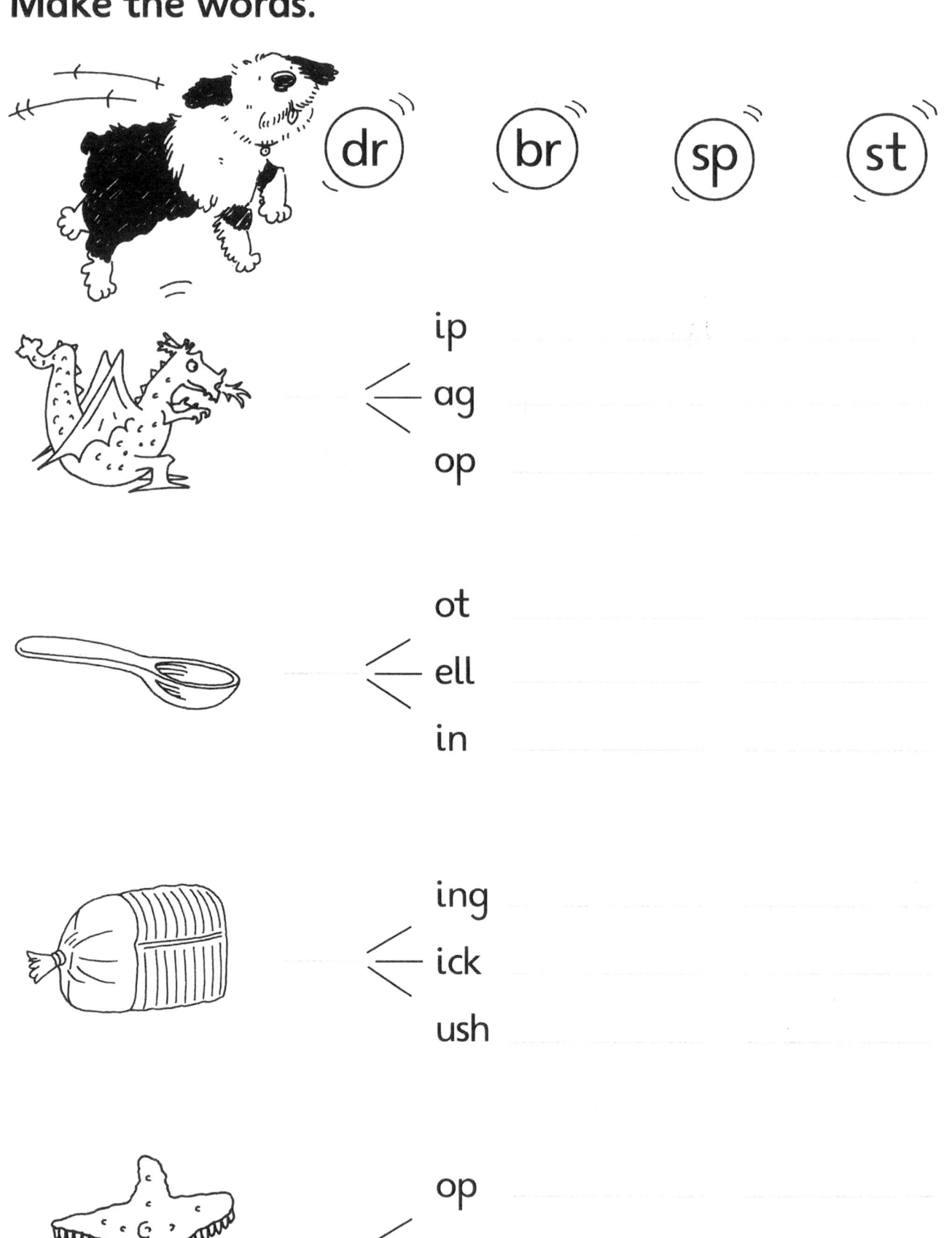

dr   br   sp   st

ip
ag
op

ot
ell
in

ing
ick
ush

op
ep
ill

Bouncer comes to stay

Skill: Identifying initial blends which have one consonant in common
Instructions: Write the blend next to the picture. Then use the blend and endings to make words and write the words twice.

Make the words.

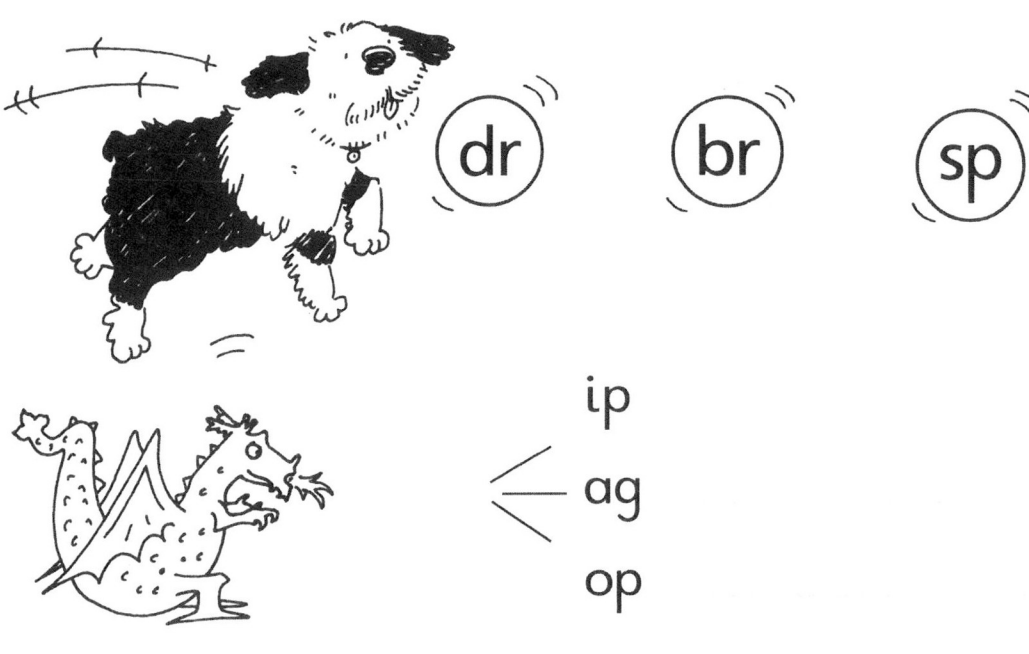

dr   br   sp   st

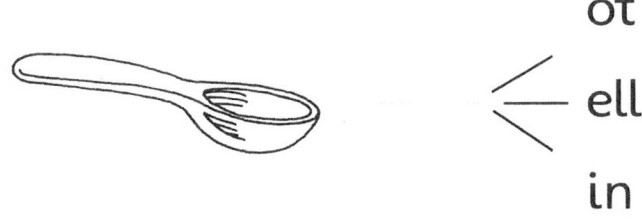

ip
ag
op

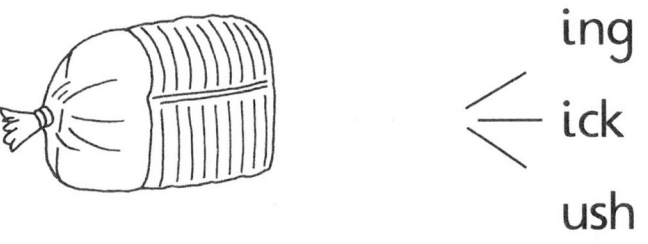

ot
ell
in

ing
ick
ush

op
ep
ill

Bouncer comes to stay

Skill: Identifying initial blends which have one consonant in common
Instructions: Write the blend next to the picture. Then use the blend and endings to make words and write the words twice.

Fill in the gaps.

been   asked   next   after   took   because   with
lots   must   came   cross   When   have   please

One day Gran _____ over to see Robin and Sally.

'Will you look _____ Bouncer for me?' she asked.

'Oh, _____ say yes, Mum!' said Robin and Sally.

Mum said, 'You will _____ to look after him.'

Sally and Robin _____ Bouncer for a walk in the park.

The _____ day Robin didn't want to walk Bouncer _____ it was too cold.

So Mum had to go for a walk _____ Bouncer.

Mum was _____ . 'If you have a dog you _____ look after it,' she said.

So Sally and Robin took Bouncer for _____ of walks.

_____ Gran came to get Bouncer, Mum said, 'Robin and Sally have _____ very good.'

Robin and Sally _____ Mum, 'Can we have a dog now?'

Bouncer comes to stay

Skill: Reading comprehension – cloze
Instructions: Look back at the story and complete the sentences using the words from the box.

Change the odd word.

Robin didn't see cold Mrs Brown walking up the path.

He couldn't hop and he pushed her into the fence.

'My don't you look where you're going?' she said.

Mum said, 'Why don't you go and say lorry again?'

Cut Mrs Brown didn't come to the door.

Robin paw Mrs Brown on the rug by the TV.

She said, 'I fell over the rug and I've curt my leg.'

Robin called to his mum, 'Mrs Brown bell over.'

Mum said, 'I'll ball for help.'

An ambulance book Mrs Brown to hospital.

The next door neighbour

Skill: Reading for meaning
Instructions: Read the sentences and underline the odd word. Then write the correct word on the line.

Match the words.

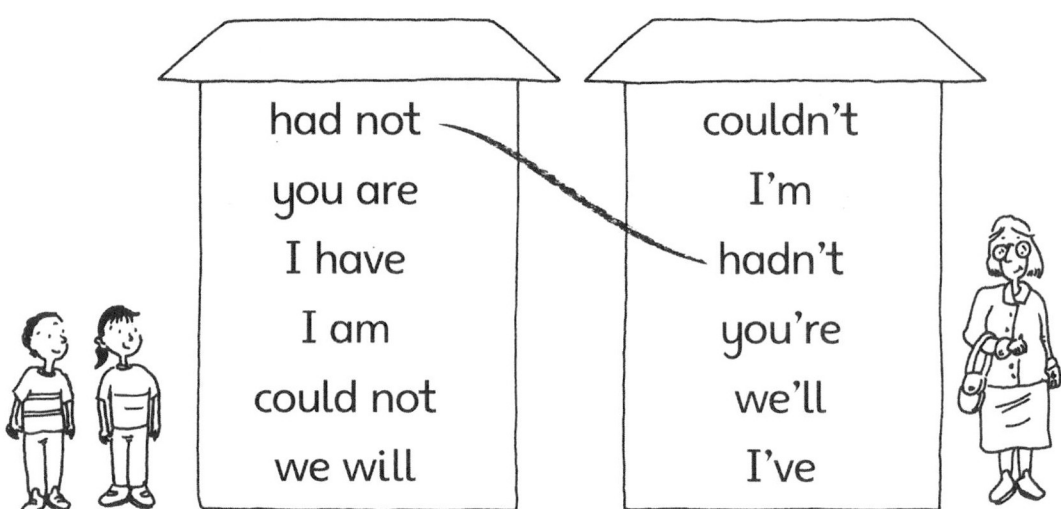

had not — couldn't
you are — I'm
I have — hadn't
I am — you're
could not — we'll
we will — I've

Make two words into one word.

'I am coming to get you,' said Sally.

Robin saw Mrs Brown but he just could not stop.

'What do you think you are doing?' said Mrs Brown.

'I fell over the rug and I have hurt my leg,' said Mrs Brown.

'We will go and get our mum,' called Robin.

'If you had not come to see Mrs Brown she could have been on the floor all night,' said the policewoman.

The next door neighbour

Skill: Using the apostrophe to mark missing letters
Instructions: Join the two words to the correct contraction. Then write the correct contraction under the two words.

Circle the blend.

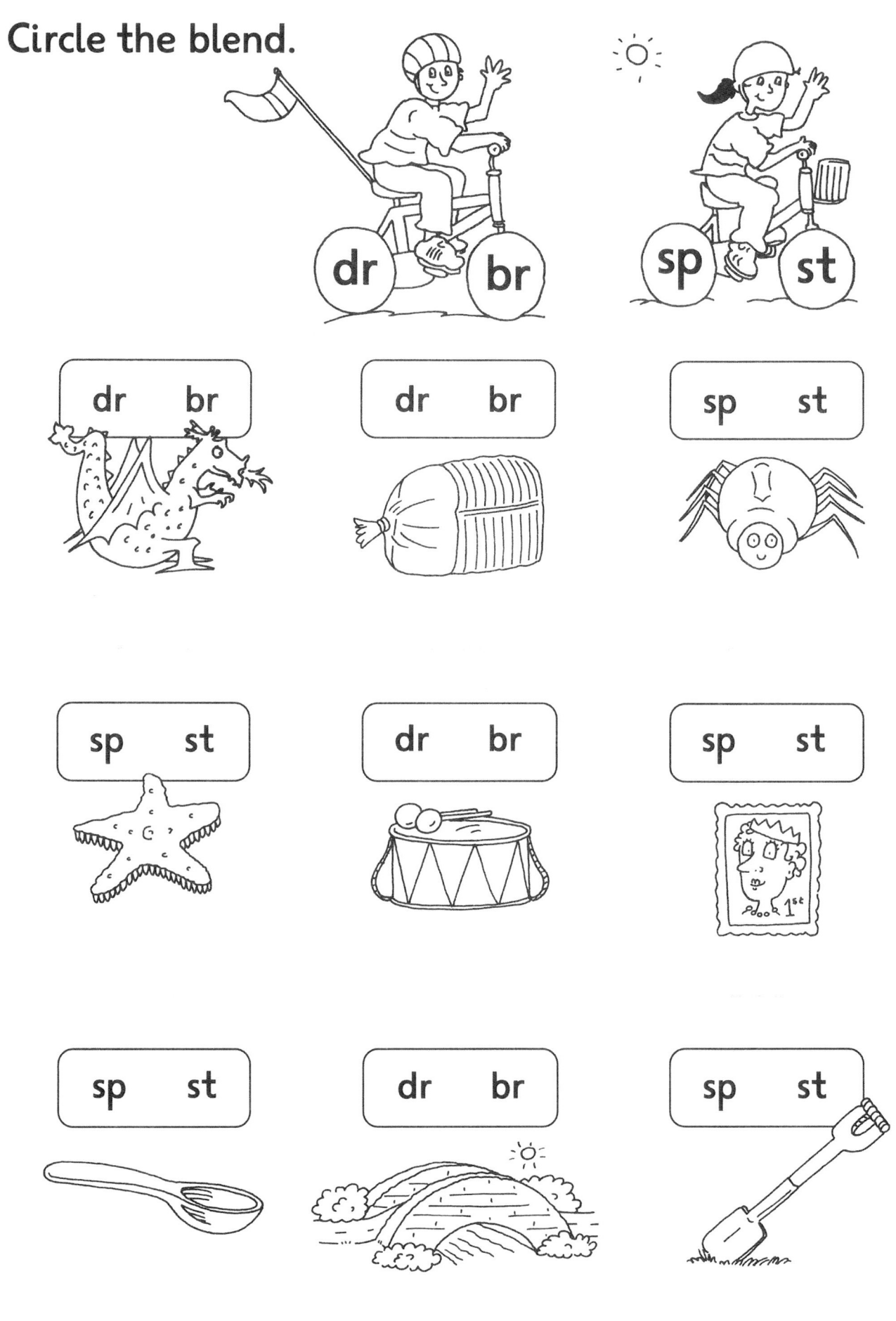

The new boy

Skill: Identifying initial blends which have one consonant in common
Instructions: Circle the correct blend above each picture and then write the blend under the picture.

Write the sentence.

Sally and Robin _____ [boy a saw a van by]

The boy said, '_____ , [with I want you don't play to]

Sally and the boy _____ [bikes on their got]

The boy _____ [fast going too Sally was much for]

Moggy _____ [bike on didn't the his see boy coming]

The boy pulled on _____ [Moggy away and his brakes ran]

The boy said, '_____ ?' [now friends Can be we]

The new boy

Skill: Reading for meaning
Instructions: Complete the sentences by rearranging the word order so that they make sense. Remember to use a full stop at the end of each sentence.

Answer the questions.

What did Robin ask Mum? (page 3)

What did Mum say? (page 3)

How did the girl say she got the bat? (page 8)

What did Sally say when she looked at the girl's bat? (page 11)

Why did Dad put Robin's bat in the shed? (page 15)

What did Robin say to the girl? (page 16)

What did the girl say to Robin? (page 16)

The cricket bat mystery

Skill: Comprehension
Instructions: Answer the questions. Look back at the story to help you. When you have finished discuss your answers with a partner.

Robin and Sally stories
Stage 7

Name

Read and do.

Draw a cricket bat in the girl's hand.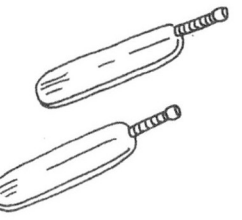

Draw a cricket bat in Dad's hand.

Draw a cricket ball on the grass.

Draw a bird in the tree.

Draw the sun in the sky.

Draw Moggy on the wall.

The cricket bat mystery

Skill: Reading and following instructions
Instructions: Read the sentences and then complete the picture.

Make the words.

(dr)   (br)   (sp)   (st)

ip
ag
op

ot
ell
in

ing
ick
ush

op
ep
ill

Bouncer comes to stay

Skill: Identifying initial blends which have one consonant in common
Instructions: Write the blend next to the picture. Then use the blend and endings to make words and write the words twice.

Fill in the gaps.

been asked next after took because with
lots must came cross When have please

One day Gran _____ over to see Robin and Sally.

'Will you look _____ Bouncer for me?' she asked.

'Oh, _____ say yes, Mum!' said Robin and Sally.

Mum said, 'You will _____ to look after him.'

Sally and Robin _____ Bouncer for a walk in the park.

The _____ day Robin didn't want to walk Bouncer _____ it was too cold.

So Mum had to go for a walk _____ Bouncer.

Mum was _____. 'If you have a dog you _____ look after it,' she said.

So Sally and Robin took Bouncer for _____ of walks.

_____ Gran came to get Bouncer, Mum said, 'Robin and Sally have _____ very good.'

Robin and Sally _____ Mum, 'Can we have a dog now?'

Bouncer comes to stay

Skill: Reading comprehension – cloze
Instructions: Look back at the story and complete the sentences using the words from the box.

Change the odd word.

Robin didn't see cold Mrs Brown walking up the path.

He couldn't hop and he pushed her into the fence.

'My don't you look where you're going?' she said.

Mum said, 'Why don't you go and say lorry again?'

Cut Mrs Brown didn't come to the door.

Robin paw Mrs Brown on the rug by the TV.

She said, 'I fell over the rug and I've curt my leg.'

Robin called to his mum, 'Mrs Brown bell over.'

Mum said, 'I'll ball for help.'

An ambulance book Mrs Brown to hospital.

The next door neighbour

Skill: Reading for meaning
Instructions: Read the sentences and underline the odd word. Then write the correct word on the line.

Match the words.

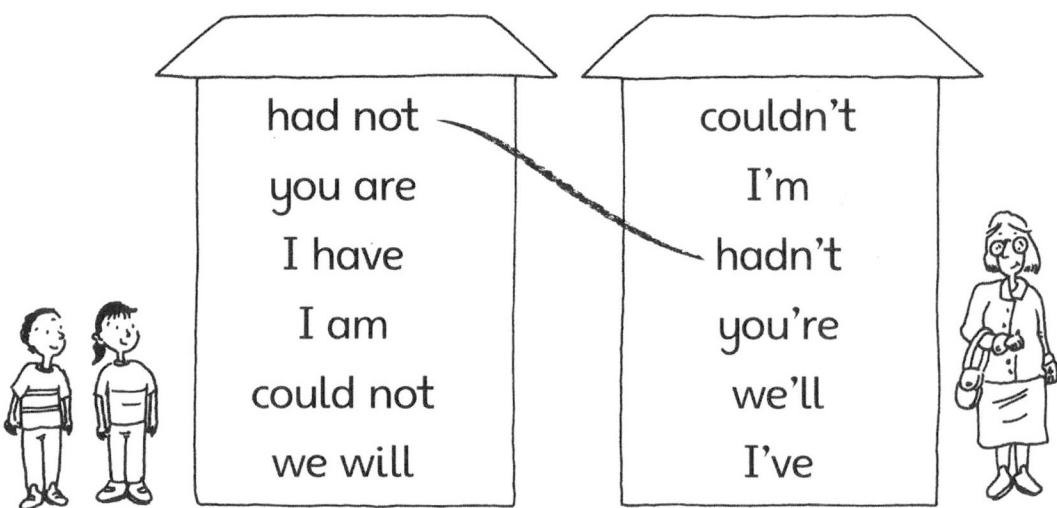

had not — hadn't
you are
I have
I am
could not
we will

couldn't
I'm
hadn't
you're
we'll
I've

Make two words into one word.

'I am coming to get you,' said Sally.

Robin saw Mrs Brown but he just could not stop.

'What do you think you are doing?' said Mrs Brown.

'I fell over the rug and I have hurt my leg,' said Mrs Brown.

'We will go and get our mum,' called Robin.

'If you had not come to see Mrs Brown she could

have been on the floor all night,' said the policewoman.

The next door neighbour

Skill: Using the apostrophe to mark missing letters
Instructions: Join the two words to the correct contraction. Then write the correct contraction under the two words.

Circle the blend.

The new boy

Skill: Identifying initial blends which have one consonant in common
Instructions: Circle the correct blend above each picture and then write the blend under the picture.

Write the sentence.

Sally and Robin _____ [boy a saw a van by]

The boy said, '_____,' [with I want you don't play to]

Sally and the boy _____ [bikes on their got]

The boy _____ [fast going too Sally was much for]

Moggy _____ [bike on didn't the his see boy coming]

The boy pulled on _____ [Moggy away and his brakes ran]

The boy said, '_____?' [now friends Can be we]

The new boy

Skill: Reading for meaning
Instructions: Complete the sentences by rearranging the word order so that they make sense. Remember to use a full stop at the end of each sentence.

Answer the questions.

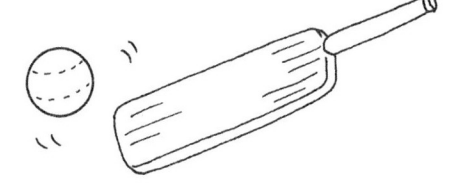

What did Robin ask Mum? (page 3)

What did Mum say? (page 3)

How did the girl say she got the bat? (page 8)

What did Sally say when she looked at the girl's bat? (page 11)

Why did Dad put Robin's bat in the shed? (page 15)

What did Robin say to the girl? (page 16)

What did the girl say to Robin? (page 16)

The cricket bat mystery

Skill: Comprehension
Instructions: Answer the questions. Look back at the story to help you. When you have finished discuss your answers with a partner.

Robin and Sally stories Stage 7

Name

Read and do.

Draw a cricket bat in the girl's hand.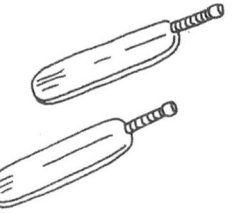

Draw a cricket bat in Dad's hand.

Draw a cricket ball on the grass.

Draw a bird in the tree.

Draw the sun in the sky.

Draw Moggy on the wall.

The cricket bat mystery

Skill: Reading and following instructions
Instructions: Read the sentences and then complete the picture.

Make the words.

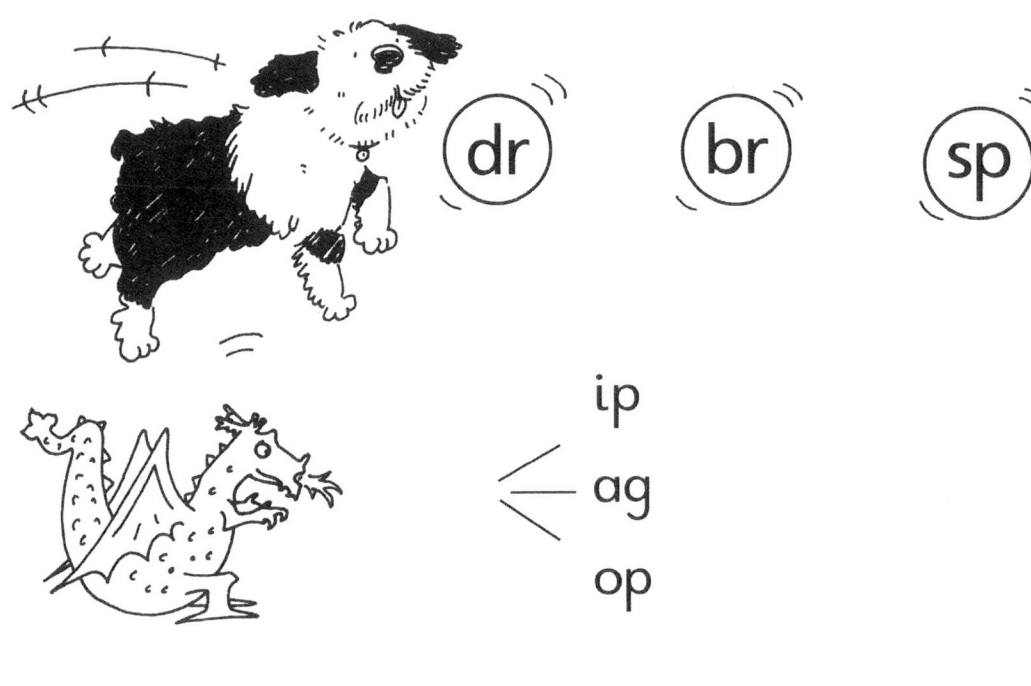

dr   br   sp   st

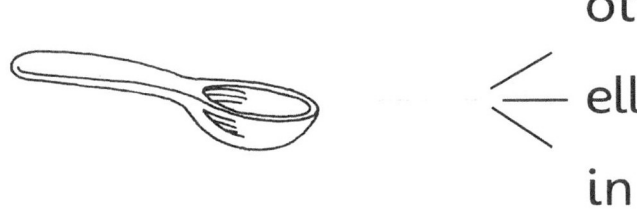

ip
ag
op

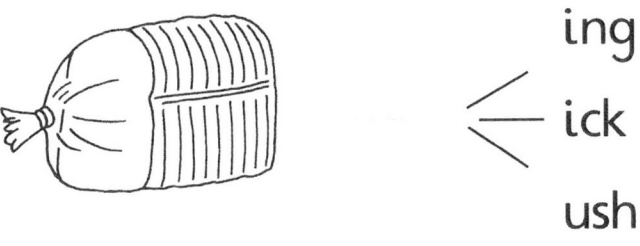

ot
ell
in

ing
ick
ush

op
ep
ill

Bouncer comes to stay

Skill: Identifying initial blends which have one consonant in common
Instructions: Write the blend next to the picture. Then use the blend and endings to make words and write the words twice.

Fill in the gaps.

been   asked   next   after   took   because   with
lots   must   came   cross   When   have   please

One day Gran _____ over to see Robin and Sally.

'Will you look _____ Bouncer for me?' she asked.

'Oh, _____ say yes, Mum!' said Robin and Sally.

Mum said, 'You will _____ to look after him.'

Sally and Robin _____ Bouncer for a walk in the park.

The _____ day Robin didn't want to walk Bouncer _____ it was too cold.

So Mum had to go for a walk _____ Bouncer.

Mum was _____ . 'If you have a dog you _____ look after it,' she said.

So Sally and Robin took Bouncer for _____ of walks.

_____ Gran came to get Bouncer, Mum said, 'Robin and Sally have _____ very good.'

Robin and Sally _____ Mum, 'Can we have a dog now?'

Bouncer comes to stay

Skill: Reading comprehension – cloze
Instructions: Look back at the story and complete the sentences using the words from the box.

Change the odd word.

Robin didn't see cold Mrs Brown walking up the path.

He couldn't hop and he pushed her into the fence.

'My don't you look where you're going?' she said.

Mum said, 'Why don't you go and say lorry again?'

Cut Mrs Brown didn't come to the door.

Robin paw Mrs Brown on the rug by the TV.

She said, 'I fell over the rug and I've curt my leg.'

Robin called to his mum, 'Mrs Brown bell over.'

Mum said, 'I'll ball for help.'

An ambulance book Mrs Brown to hospital.

The next door neighbour

Skill: Reading for meaning
Instructions: Read the sentences and underline the odd word. Then write the correct word on the line.

Match the words.

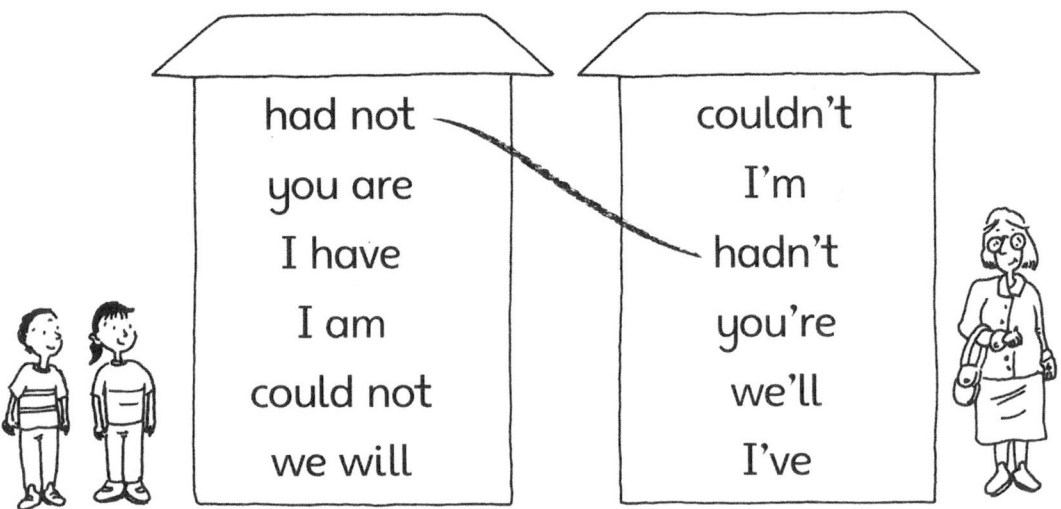

had not — hadn't
you are — you're
I have — I've
I am — I'm
could not — couldn't
we will — we'll

Make two words into one word.

'I am coming to get you,' said Sally.

Robin saw Mrs Brown but he just could not stop.

'What do you think you are doing?' said Mrs Brown.

'I fell over the rug and I have hurt my leg,' said Mrs Brown.

'We will go and get our mum,' called Robin.

'If you had not come to see Mrs Brown she could

have been on the floor all night,' said the policewoman.

The next door neighbour

Skill: Using the apostrophe to mark missing letters
Instructions: Join the two words to the correct contraction. Then write the correct contraction under the two words.

Circle the blend.

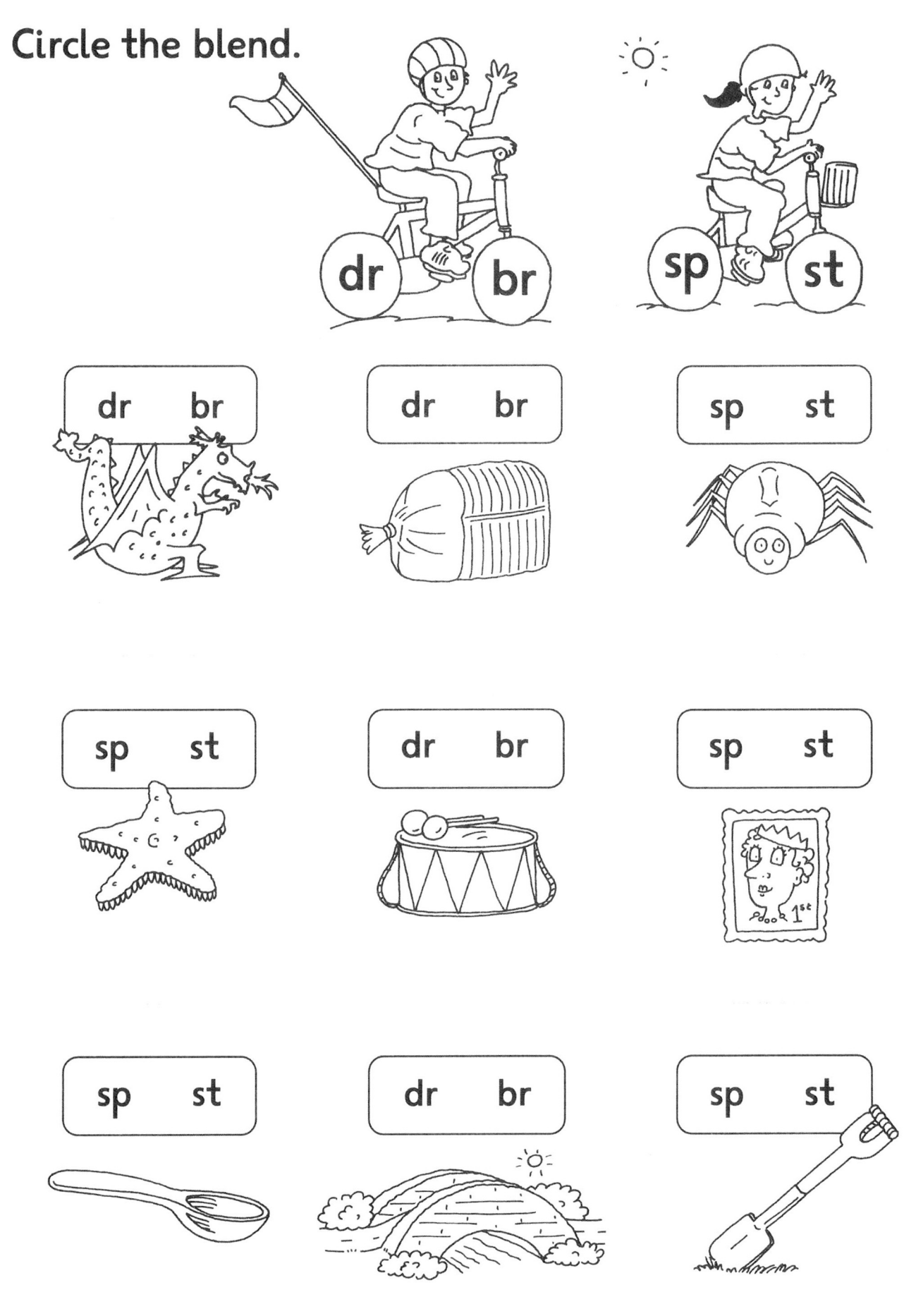

The new boy

Skill: Identifying initial blends which have one consonant in common
Instructions: Circle the correct blend above each picture and then write the blend under the picture.

Write the sentence.

Sally and Robin _____ [saw a boy by a van]

The boy said, '_____,' [I don't want you to play with]

Sally and the boy _____ [got on their bikes]

The boy _____ [was going too fast for Sally]

Moggy _____ [didn't see the boy coming on his bike]

The boy pulled on _____ [his brakes and Moggy ran away]

The boy said, '_____?' [Can we be friends now]

The new boy

Skill: Reading for meaning
Instructions: Complete the sentences by rearranging the word order so that they make sense. Remember to use a full stop at the end of each sentence.

3

Answer the questions.

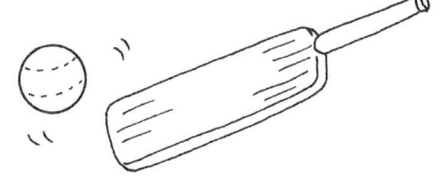

What did Robin ask Mum? (page 3)

What did Mum say? (page 3)

How did the girl say she got the bat? (page 8)

What did Sally say when she looked at the girl's bat? (page 11)

Why did Dad put Robin's bat in the shed? (page 15)

What did Robin say to the girl? (page 16)

What did the girl say to Robin? (page 16)

The cricket bat mystery

Skill: Comprehension
Instructions: Answer the questions. Look back at the story to help you. When you have finished discuss your answers with a partner.

Robin and Sally stories Stage 7

Name

Read and do.

Draw a cricket bat in the girl's hand.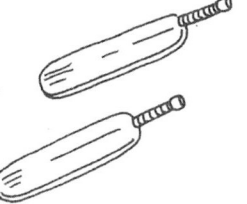

Draw a cricket bat in Dad's hand.

Draw a cricket ball on the grass.

Draw a bird in the tree.

Draw the sun in the sky.

Draw Moggy on the wall.

The cricket bat mystery

Skill: Reading and following instructions
Instructions: Read the sentences and then complete the picture.

Make the words.

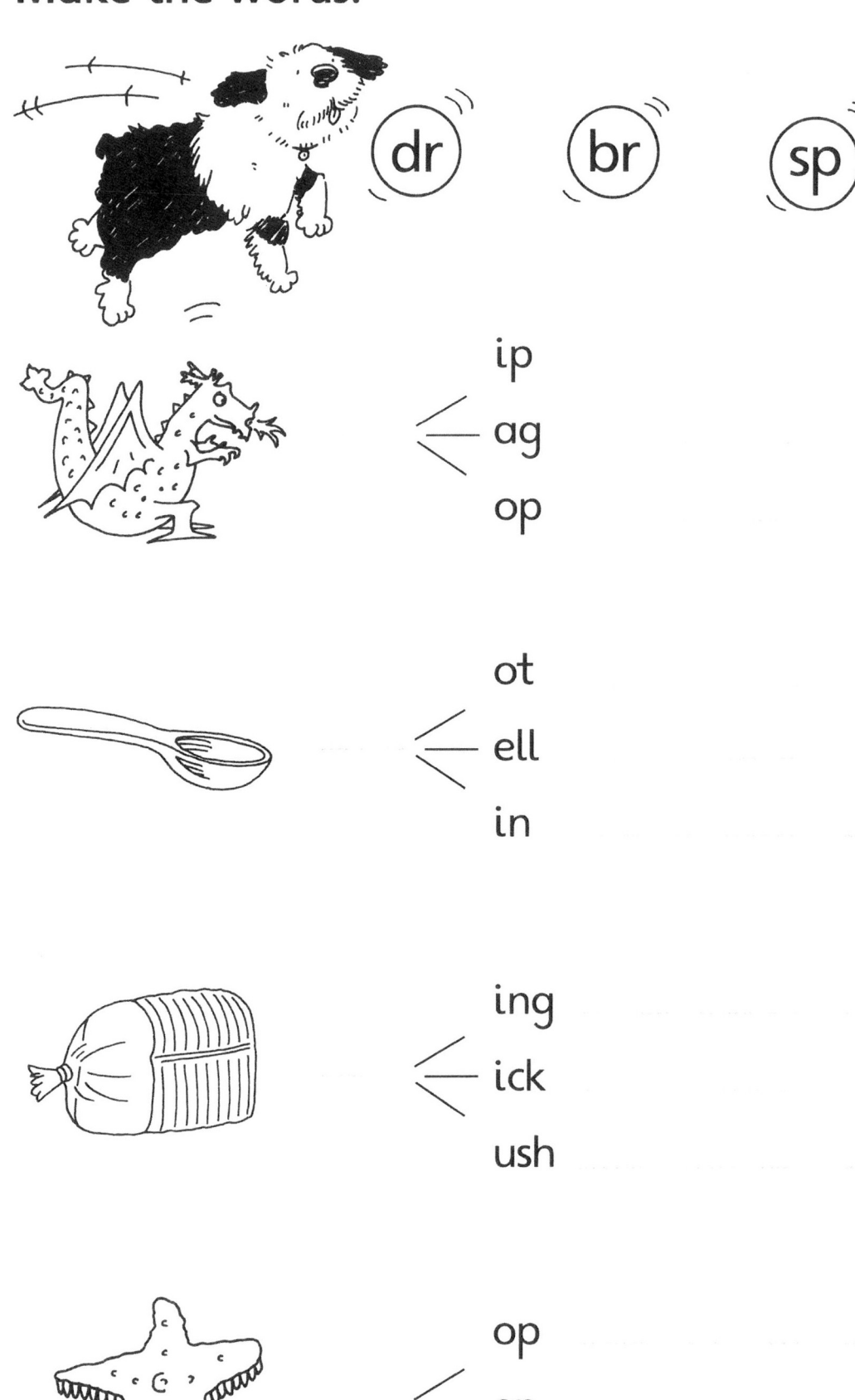

dr   br   sp   st

ip
ag
op

ot
ell
in

ing
ick
ush

op
ep
ill

Bouncer comes to stay

Skill: Identifying initial blends which have one consonant in common
Instructions: Write the blend next to the picture. Then use the blend and endings to make words and write the words twice.

Fill in the gaps.

been asked next after took because with
lots must came cross When have please

One day Gran _____ over to see Robin and Sally.

'Will you look _____ Bouncer for me?' she asked.

'Oh, _____ say yes, Mum!' said Robin and Sally.

Mum said, 'You will _____ to look after him.'

Sally and Robin _____ Bouncer for a walk in the park.

The _____ day Robin didn't want to walk Bouncer _____ it was too cold.

So Mum had to go for a walk _____ Bouncer.

Mum was _____ . 'If you have a dog you _____ look after it,' she said.

So Sally and Robin took Bouncer for _____ of walks.

_____ Gran came to get Bouncer, Mum said, 'Robin and Sally have _____ very good.'

Robin and Sally _____ Mum, 'Can we have a dog now?'

Bouncer comes to stay

Skill: Reading comprehension – cloze
Instructions: Look back at the story and complete the sentences using the words from the box.

Change the odd word.

Robin didn't see cold Mrs Brown walking up the path.

He couldn't hop and he pushed her into the fence.

'My don't you look where you're going?' she said.

Mum said, 'Why don't you go and say lorry again?'

Cut Mrs Brown didn't come to the door.

Robin paw Mrs Brown on the rug by the TV.

She said, 'I fell over the rug and I've curt my leg.'

Robin called to his mum, 'Mrs Brown bell over.'

Mum said, 'I'll ball for help.'

An ambulance book Mrs Brown to hospital.

The next door neighbour

Skill: Reading for meaning
Instructions: Read the sentences and underline the odd word. Then write the correct word on the line.

Match the words.

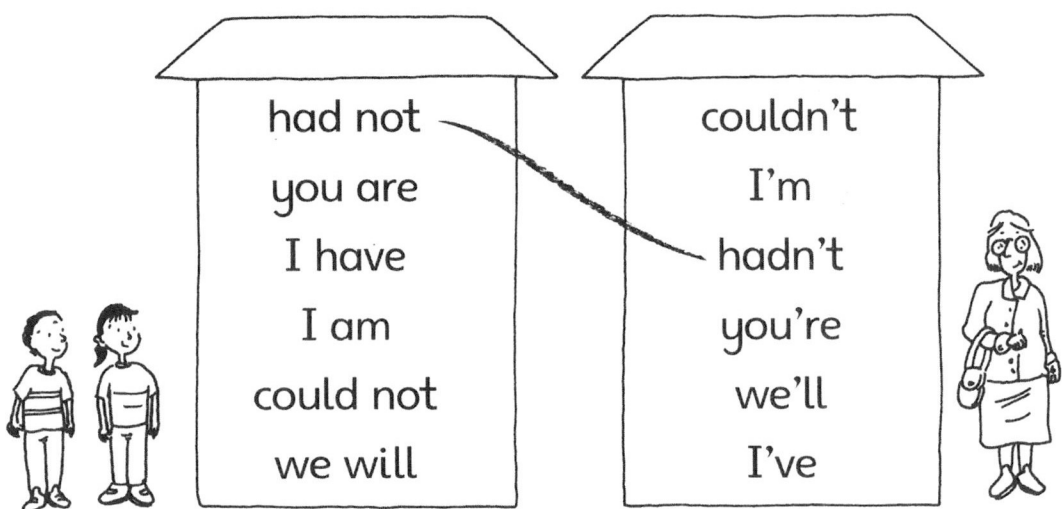

had not	couldn't
you are	I'm
I have	hadn't
I am	you're
could not	we'll
we will	I've

Make two words into one word.

'I am coming to get you,' said Sally.

Robin saw Mrs Brown but he just could not stop.

'What do you think you are doing?' said Mrs Brown.

'I fell over the rug and I have hurt my leg,' said Mrs Brown.

'We will go and get our mum,' called Robin.

'If you had not come to see Mrs Brown she could

have been on the floor all night,' said the policewoman.

The next door neighbour

Skill: Using the apostrophe to mark missing letters
Instructions: Join the two words to the correct contraction. Then write the correct contraction under the two words.

Circle the blend.

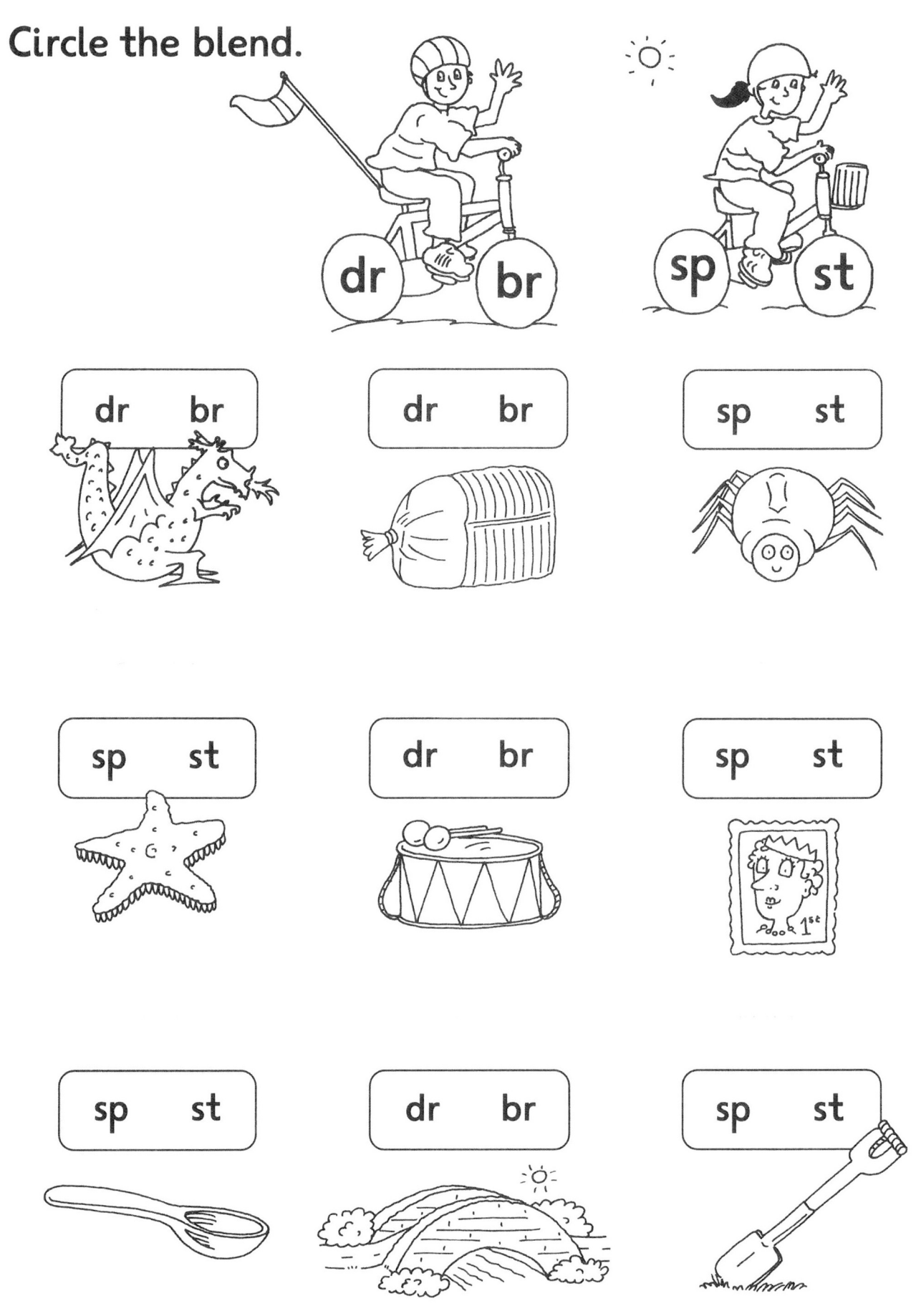

The new boy

Skill: Identifying initial blends which have one consonant in common
Instructions: Circle the correct blend above each picture and then write the blend under the picture.

Write the sentence.

Sally and Robin saw a boy by a van.

The boy said, 'I don't want you to play with,'

Sally and the boy got on their bikes.

The boy was going too fast for Sally.

Moggy didn't see the boy coming on his bike.

The boy pulled on his brakes and Moggy ran away.

The boy said, 'Can we be friends now?'

The new boy

Skill: Reading for meaning
Instructions: Complete the sentences by rearranging the word order so that they make sense. Remember to use a full stop at the end of each sentence.

Answer the questions.

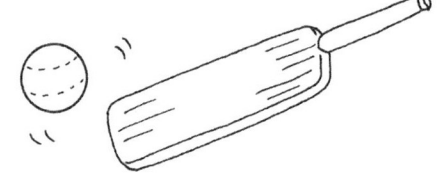

What did Robin ask Mum? (page 3)

What did Mum say? (page 3)

How did the girl say she got the bat? (page 8)

What did Sally say when she looked at the girl's bat? (page 11)

Why did Dad put Robin's bat in the shed? (page 15)

What did Robin say to the girl? (page 16)

What did the girl say to Robin? (page 16)

The cricket bat mystery

Skill: Comprehension
Instructions: Answer the questions. Look back at the story to help you. When you have finished discuss your answers with a partner.

Robin and Sally stories
Stage 7

Name

Read and do.

Draw a cricket bat in the girl's hand.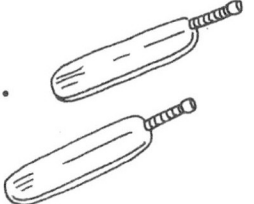

Draw a cricket bat in Dad's hand.

Draw a cricket ball on the grass.

Draw a bird in the tree.

Draw the sun in the sky.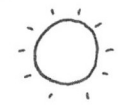

Draw Moggy on the wall.

The cricket bat mystery

Skill: Reading and following instructions
Instructions: Read the sentences and then complete the picture.